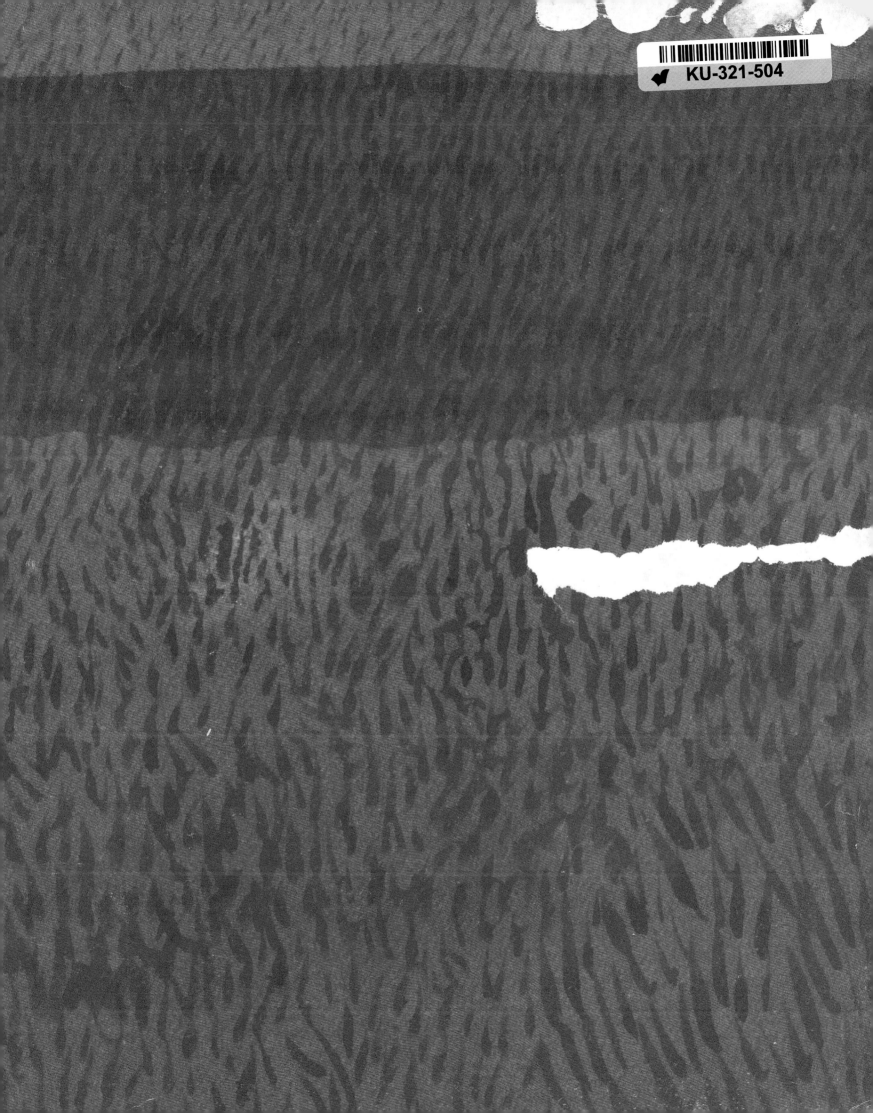

Voices
IN THE PARK

Anthony Browne

DOUBLEDAY

London · New York · Toronto · Sydney · Auckland

TRANSWORLD PUBLISHERS LTD
61-63 Uxbridge Road, London W5 5SA

TRANSWORLD PUBLISHERS (AUSTRALIA) PTY LTD
15-25 Helles Avenue, Moorebank, NSW 2170

TRANSWORLD PUBLISHERS (NZ) LTD
3 William Pickering Drive, Albany, Auckland

DOUBLEDAY CANADA LTD
105 Bond Street, Toronto, Ontario M5B 1Y3

Published in 1998 by Doubleday
a division of Transworld Publishers Ltd

A catalogue record for this book is available
from the British Library

ISBN 0 385 408587

Printed in Italy

It was time to take Victoria, our pedigree Labrador, and Charles, our son, for a walk.

When we arrived at the park,
I let Victoria off her lead.
Immediately some scruffy
mongrel appeared and started
bothering her. I shooed it off,
but the horrible thing chased
her all over the park.

I ordered it to go away, but it took no notice of me whatsoever. "Sit," I said to Charles. "Here."

I was just planning what we should have to eat
that evening when I saw Charles had
disappeared. Oh dear! Where had he gone?

You get some frightful
types in the park these
days! I called his name for
what seemed like an age.

Then I saw him talking to
a very rough-looking child.
"Charles, come here. At
once!" I said. "And come
here please, Victoria."

We walked home in silence.

I needed to get out of the house, so me and Smudge took the dog to the park.

**He loves it there. I wish I
had half the energy he's got.**

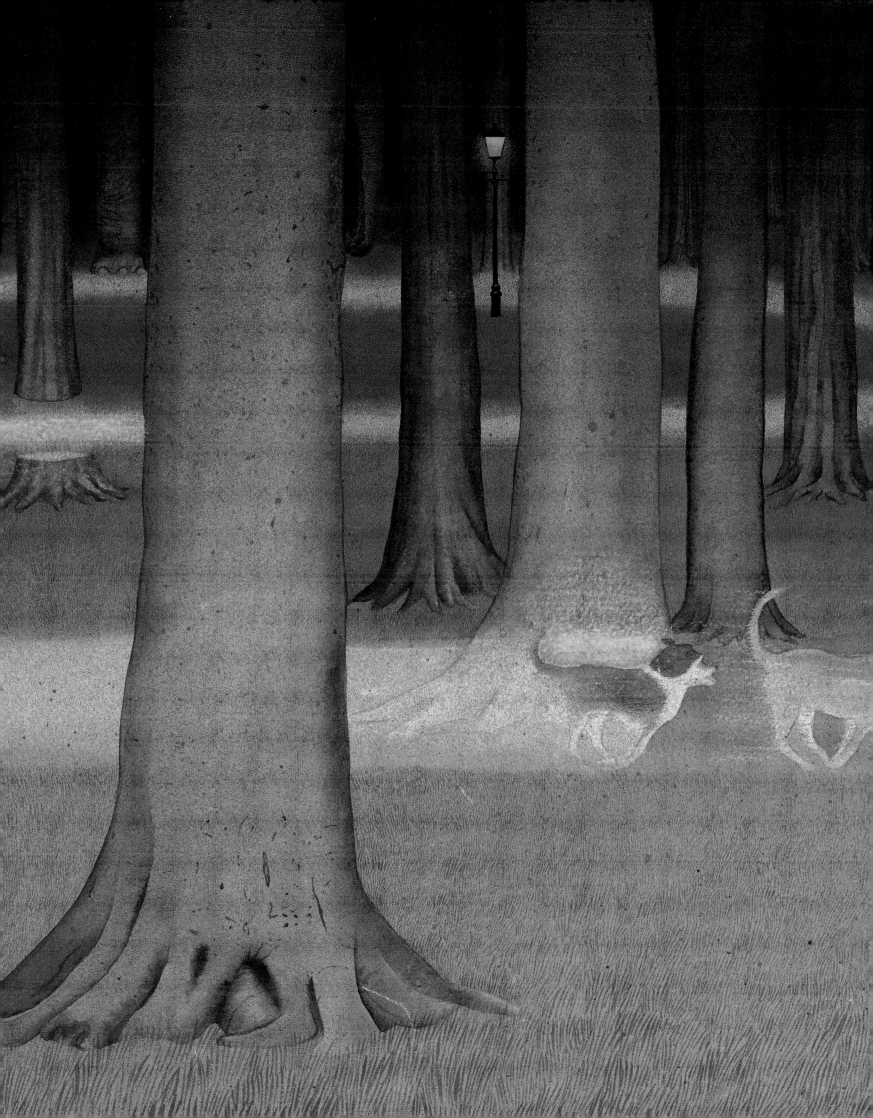

I settled on a bench and looked through the paper for a job. I know it's a waste of time really, but you've got to have a bit of hope, haven't you?

Then it was time to go. Smudge cheered me up. She chatted happily to me all the way home.

I was at home on my own again.
It's so boring. Then Mummy said
that it was time for our walk.

There was a very friendly dog in the park and
Victoria was having a great time. I wished I was.

"D'you wanna come on the slide?"
a voice asked. It was a girl,
unfortunately, but I went anyway.
She was brilliant on the slide, she
went really fast. I was amazed.

The two dogs raced round like old friends.

The girl took off her
coat and swung on
the climbing frame,
so I did the same.

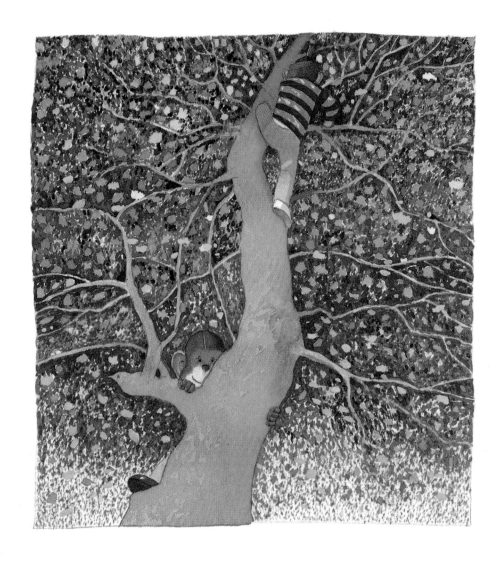

I'm good at climbing trees,
so I showed her how to do it.
She told me her name was
Smudge – a funny name, I know,
but she's quite nice. Then
Mummy caught us talking
together and I had to go home.

Maybe Smudge will be there next time?

Dad had been really fed up, so I was pleased when he said we could take **Albert** to the park.

Albert's always in such a hurry to be let off his lead. He went straight up to this lovely dog and sniffed its bum (he always does that). Of course, the other dog didn't mind, but its owner was really angry, the silly twit.

I got talking to this boy. I thought he
was a bit of a wimp at first, but he's
okay. We played on the see-saw and
he didn't say much, but later on he
was a bit more friendly.

We both burst out
laughing when we saw
Albert having a swim.

Then we all played on
the bandstand, and I felt
really, really happy.

Charlie picked a flower
and gave it to me.

Then his mum called
him and he had to go.
He looked sad.

When I got home I put the flower in some water, and made Dad a nice cup of tea.